Crab,

Dab

& Blenny

This book belongs to ....

**This book is dedicated to
Leigh, who loves exploring the outdoors and
discovering the many wonders of the natural world,
and Amelie C, who adores swimming
in the sea with her Grandma**

www.dogpigeon.co.uk

First published in 2021 by Dogpigeon Books

ISBN 978-0-9956465-4-4

Dab, he was old-fashioned,
Thought the rockpool was just fine.
He liked its sandy bottom
And its clear and cooling brine.
He felt protected by the rock,
The shadow that it cast:
A shelter from the sea beyond;
So strong, so cold, so vast.

But Crab, he was, well, crabby.
He didn't like his home,
Was jealous of the bigger crabs,
With longer legs to roam.
He scorned his quiet neighbours,
Blenny, Dab and Prawn,
Thought Limpet was a sucker,
Anemone, a yawn.

Crab and Dab, they both enjoyed
The visitors who came
To the pool at high tide;
No two days were the same.

It might be playful gobies...

A starfish...

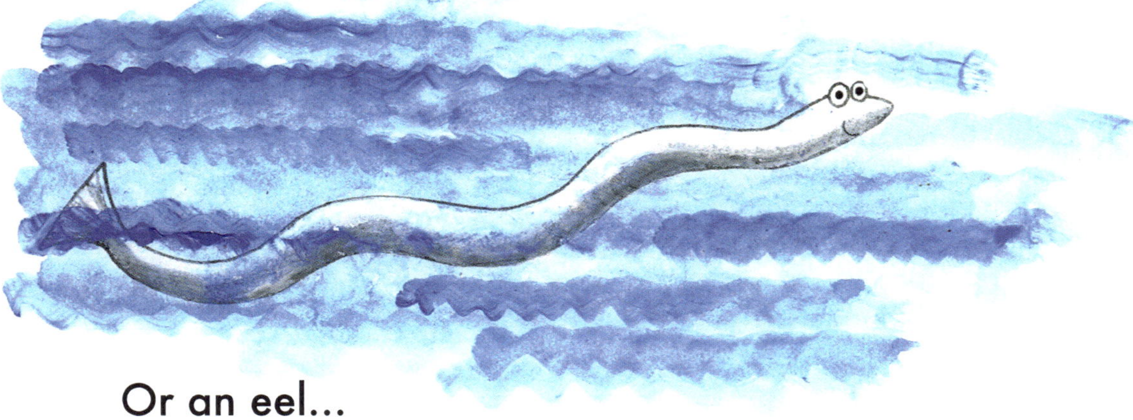

Or an eel...

A scorpion fish...

Or pipefish,
With its slippery-slidey feel.

But on the day 'The Thing' washed in,
The rockpool was quite split.
Dab and Blenny were put out,
But Crab, he welcomed it.
He loved its shine and colour,
He thought it rather cool
To have a piece of plastic
To brighten up the pool!

Imagine, then, the thrill he felt when,
At the next high tide,
Another object floated in,
With space for him inside.
At last he'd have a stylish home;
A modern place to dwell.
He couldn't wait to get inside
And ditch his tired old shell.

Blenny laughed at Crab's new home.
Prawn thought it absurd.
Limpet, the strong, silent type,
Never said a word.
But Dab, he was a kindly fish,
And happy for his friend;
Kept his worries to himself,
Not wanting to offend.

So, over time, the rockpool
Took on a different form.
Shells and seaweeds were more rare
And man-made was the norm.
The crab, of course, embraced the change,
Loved all things bright and new.
The others missed the Peacock's Tail,
The Kelp and Gutweed too.

Though more was changing in the pool
Than things that could be seen;
Looking from their fish-eye lens,
The water still seemed clean.
But hidden from the watchful eyes
Of Prawn and Dab and Blenny,
A host of plastic microbeads –
So tiny, but so many.

The rockpool was polluted,
The water was not clean,
Filled with specks of plastic,
Too minute to be seen:
Microbeads from toothpaste;
Clothing fibre too;
Ground up bits of plastic,
All floating in the blue.

All this was invisible to
Good friends, Prawn and Dab,
To Blenny and to Limpet,
Anemone and Crab.
But though they couldn't see it,
It washed across their skin,
And though they couldn't taste it,
They drank the plastic in.

So life within the rockpool
Continued as before,
Despite increasing clutter
Across its sandy floor.
The crab still got excited
When new junk floated in,
The dab, he still said nothing,
Just flicked a wary fin.

Then one day, very early,
Dab was woken by a cry,
A kerfuffle, a commotion;
He set out to find out why...
And then he saw, to his dismay,
Blenny trapped in twine;
Trussed up tight and twisted
In the orange plastic line.

Dab did his best to help his friend
To get out of the bind,
He tried to free him from the line,
But Blenny stayed entwined.
By now, the other rockpool friends
Were looking on, alarmed:
Even if he got away,
Would Blenny be unharmed?

But then the Crab stepped forward,
Said: “I’ve told you all before:
If you ever have a problem,
All you need’s a trusty claw.”
He scuttled up to Blenny,
Gave the line a snip,
Then, when that didn’t cut it,
Took it in his grip...

He pulled and tugged and twisted,
But the line stayed tightly bound.
Exhausted by the effort,
Blenny sank down to the ground.

The friends looked on, despairing,
Not knowing what to do,
And as the daylight faded,
Their fears just grew and grew.

Then early the next morning,
They got another shock:
A sudden surge of water
Smashed them all against the rock.
At first they were too dazed to see,
But as the water cleared,

The outline of a large pink foot,
Gradually appeared.

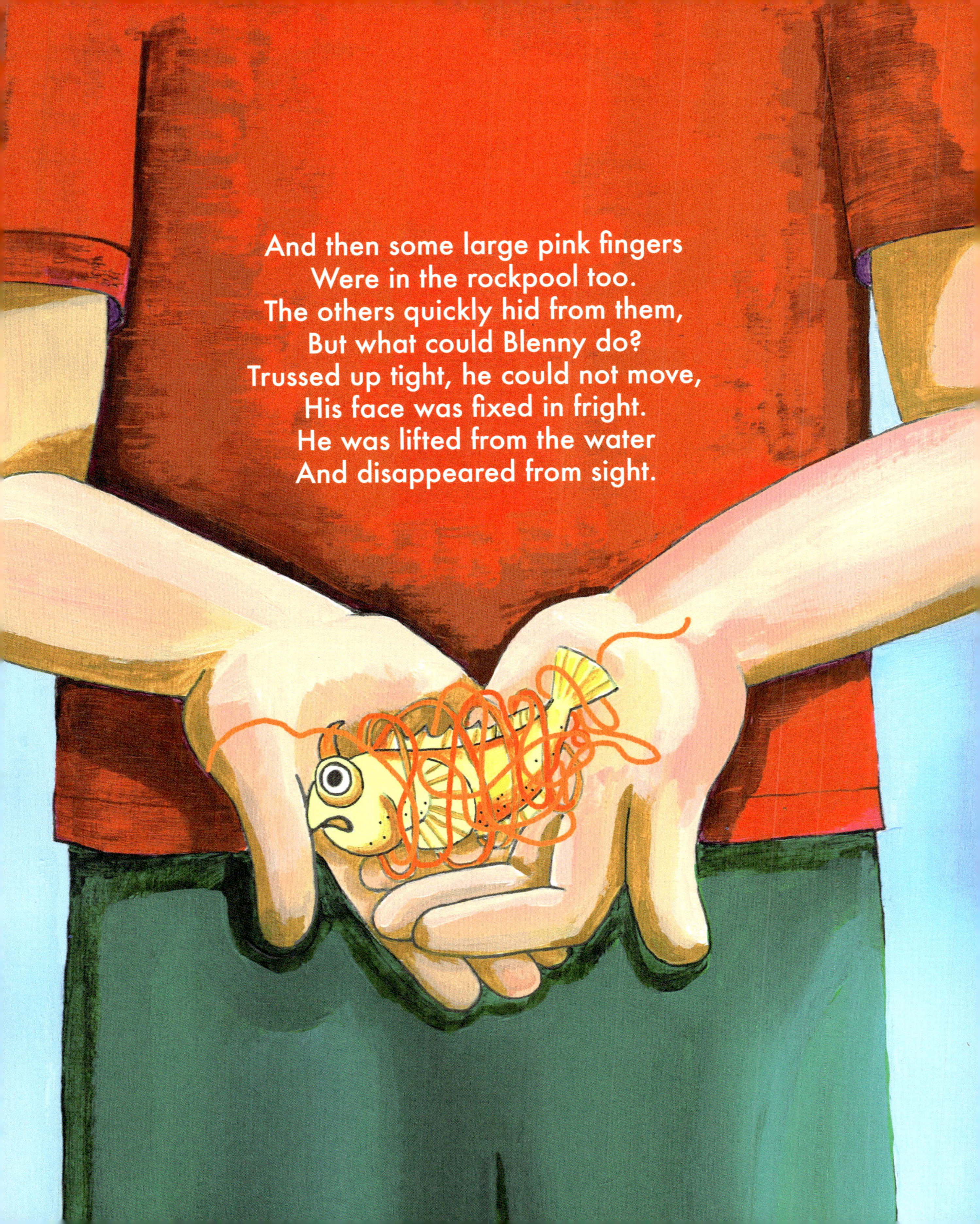

And then some large pink fingers
Were in the rockpool too.
The others quickly hid from them,
But what could Blenny do?
Trussed up tight, he could not move,
His face was fixed in fright.
He was lifted from the water
And disappeared from sight.

There was panic in the rockpool.
Poor Blenny had been taken!
Fearing he was gone for good,
His friends were sad and shaken.

And when the hand appeared again,
They thought it was the end...
Until the fingers opened
And released their grateful friend.

Crab gave out a little cry
As plastic was removed.

But Dab and Prawn and Blenny,
They all thoroughly approved.
They were happy for their rockpool,
To return to shells and weed...

And one day, quite soon after,
Even Crab agreed.

The rockpool in *Crab, Dab & Blenny* is based
on these real rockpools in St Helens, on the Isle of Wight

Also by Peta Rainford
The Niggle
Jacob Starke Loves The Dark
Hairy Fairy
Isabella, Rotten Speller
Isabella's Adventures in Numberland
Jamie and the Joke Factory
Milly's Marvellous Mistakes

www.dogpigeon.co.uk

Printed in Great Britain
by Amazon

61065421R00020